How to Write a Bestselling Billionaire Romance

From Character Creation to Market Domination

Just Bae

Contents

Introduction

The billionaire romance genre is a dazzling realm where fantasy meets reality in the most extravagant ways. It's a world where wealth and power are the backdrops to tales of passion, love, and emotional growth. This genre captivates readers with stories of alpha heroes, often billionaires, who are powerful yet vulnerable, meeting their match in partners who challenge and complement them. The allure of luxury combined with deep emotional connections makes these stories irresistible. Authors like J.S. Scott and Sylvia Day have mastered the art of weaving compelling narratives that transport readers into a world where love knows no bounds and every luxury is within reach.

Understanding reader expectations in the billionaire romance genre is crucial for any author aspiring to make their mark. Readers come with specific anticipations: a blend of fantasy, escapism, intense emotional journeys, and the attraction of the billionaire lifestyle. They seek characters with depth and complexity, plots that offer tension and satisfaction, and settings that evoke a sense of grandeur and luxury. Crafting a story that meets these expectations requires a delicate balance. It's about creating a narrative that offers escape while remaining grounded in the emotional truths that resonate with the reader's experiences and desires.

The formula behind a bestselling romance novel, particularly in the billionaire genre, isn't about adhering to a rigid set of rules but understanding the elements that resonate with readers. At its core, a bestselling romance novel features compelling characters who undergo significant growth, an engaging plot with just the right amount of tension and conflict, and a setting that enriches the narrative. The chemistry between the main characters must be palpable, their emotional journey believable, and their eventual union satisfying and well-earned. Incorporating the billionaire element adds an additional layer of fantasy and aspiration, elevating the romance's stakes and allure.

Billionaire romances often hinge on the dynamic between the powerful, frequently enigmatic billionaire and their love interest, who brings a sense of normalcy, challenge, or new perspective to the billionaire's life. This contrast is a key driver of the genre's appeal, offering readers a glimpse into a life of luxury while grounding the story in universal themes of love, redemption, and personal growth. With their complex layers and hidden vulnerabilities, the billionaire character becomes a canvas for exploring themes of power, responsibility, and the transformative power of love.

The settings in these novels are not just backgrounds but integral components of the story. They provide a canvas on which the romance unfolds, from luxurious penthouses and exotic beaches to private jets and lavish galas. These settings contribute to the fantasy, offering readers an escape into a world of beauty and extravagance. However, the most successful authors ensure that the emotional landscape of their characters is just as rich and compelling as the physical one, grounding the luxury with a sense of authenticity and relatability.

The emotional journey in billionaire romances is paramount. Readers are drawn to the genre not just by the trappings of wealth but by the emotional depth and development of the characters. The path to love is often fraught with obstacles, misunderstandings, and personal growth, making the eventual happy ending all the more satisfying. This journey reflects the readers' desires and fears, allowing them to experience, vicariously, the challenges and triumphs of love.

The attraction of the billionaire romance genre lies in its ability to blend fantasy with reality. The billionaire character, often portrayed with invincibility and vulnerability, offers a unique fantasy — the idea that love can break through barriers of wealth and power. Yet, these stories remain relatable through their characters' emotional struggles and growth, reflecting the universal quest for love and understanding.

The tension and conflict in these stories often arise from the world of wealth and power itself, presenting unique challenges and stakes for the characters. It's not just about navigating a relationship but also about dealing with the implications of entering or belonging to a world vastly different from the ordinary. This tension drives the narrative forward, providing a rich ground for exploring themes of trust, sacrifice, and the true value of love.

The detailed portrayal of luxury and exclusivity drives reader engagement in the billionaire romance genre. The captivating description of settings, lifestyle, and the trappings of wealth serves not only to create a vivid backdrop but also to create an atmosphere of aspiration and passion. It's a celebration of the finer things in life, seen through the lens of romance.

However, the heart of a bestselling billionaire romance novel lies in its ability to tell a compelling story of emotional growth and connection. The external trappings of wealth and luxury are secondary to the internal journey of the characters. Their path to finding love and fulfillment amidst the complexities of their world is what truly captivates and keeps readers returning to the genre.

The formula for a bestselling romance, especially within this niche, also hinges on creating a sense of anticipation and payoff. The buildup of emotional and situational tension and its eventual resolution plays a crucial role in satisfying the reader's expectations. It's about crafting a journey that feels both inevitable and earned, leading to a climax that resonates with the reader on a deeply emotional level.

Incorporating elements of conflict, whether through internal struggles, external pressures, or both, adds depth to the romance. These challenges serve to test the characters, making their growth and the strength of their bond all the more compelling. The best billionaire romances use conflict not just as a barrier to love but as a catalyst for change, driving the characters closer together as they navigate through adversity.

The role of secondary characters and subplots cannot be underestimated in enriching the narrative landscape of a billionaire romance. These elements add layers to the story, offering different perspectives on the central romance and highlighting themes of friendship, loyalty, and the impact of the past. They provide a fuller picture of the characters' world, making the story more engaging and complex.

A bestselling billionaire romance also skillfully balances the fantasy elements of the genre with moments of authenticity and relatability. This balance allows readers to dream while connecting with the characters on a human level. The stories that resonate most are those that, despite their glamorous settings, speak to the heart's deepest desires and fears.

Understanding and meeting reader expectations is about more than just following a formula. It's about creating a story that speaks to the heart and offers an escape and a reflection of the reader's dreams and desires. A bestselling billionaire romance novel transports, transforms, and touches the reader, leaving them both satisfied and yearning for more.

Chapter 1

Overview

The billionaire romance genre, a compelling segment of the broader romance literary world, captivates readers with tales of luxury, power, and the irresistible allure of love conquering all, even the mightiest of fortunes. This genre intertwines the fantasy of unimaginable wealth with the universal quest for love, creating a narrative that escapes from and mirrors real-life desires and conflicts. Take, for example, *The Marriage Bargain* by Jennifer Probst, where a marriage contract brings together a billionaire and a woman with nothing to lose, only for them to discover that love is the most valuable asset of all. These stories often follow protagonists as they navigate the complexities of high society, corporate battles, and personal demons, all while finding love in the most unexpected places.

Another hallmark of the billionaire romance genre is its ability to blend the fantasy of luxury with the emotional depth of realistic, relatable human experiences. In *Bared to You* by Sylvia Day, readers are drawn into the intricately detailed lives of two deeply flawed characters whose past traumas and present desires intertwine within the lavish backdrop of New York City's elite. Day's narrative skillfully demonstrates that universal struggles with self-worth, intimacy, and vulnerability lie beneath the glittering surface of wealth and success. These themes resonate with readers, offering an escape into a world of luxury and a reflection on personal emotional journeys.

The genre also excels in presenting characters who embody the dream of rising to the pinnacle of success while remaining grounded by the challenges and triumphs of falling in love. *Fifty Shades of Grey* by E.L. James, despite its polarizing reception, undeniably transformed the landscape of billionaire romance, spotlighting the dynamics of power, control, and vulnerability. The relationship between Christian Grey, a billionaire with a troubled past, and Anastasia Steele, a young, innocent college graduate, captivated millions by showcasing how love can emerge in the most complex of circumstances, challenging both characters to confront their deepest fears and desires.

Billionaire romances often explore the tension between the public facade of wealth and the private reality of emotional need and connection. In *The Tycoon's Revenge* by Melody

Anne, readers delve into the story of Derek Titan, a billionaire who seems to have it all but is driven by a need for revenge and redemption that only love can heal. Anne's work is a compelling example of how these narratives can peel back the layers of their characters, revealing the vulnerability beneath the surface of power and prestige.

The genre is also known for its diverse settings and contexts, from corporate boardrooms and exotic locations to small towns and secluded islands. *The Greek's Virgin Bride* by Julia James showcases an lavish world of international business and high society, where a marriage of convenience slowly unfolds into a deep, passionate love. This diversity in setting allows authors to explore different facets of the billionaire lifestyle, from the pressures of public scrutiny to the joys and challenges of navigating love amidst wealth.

Moreover, billionaire romance novels often incorporate elements of drama, mystery, and suspense, adding layers of complexity to the central love story. In *Ruthless* by Lisa Jackson, the intertwining of a suspenseful plot with a romantic core exemplifies how the genre can keep readers on the edge of their seats, both through the thrill of the unfolding mystery and the development of the romantic relationship. This blend of genres enriches the narrative, offering readers a multifaceted experience beyond traditional romance.

The appeal of the billionaire romance genre also lies in its portrayal of transformation — not just of the characters but also of their relationships and worldviews. *Managing the Bosses* by Lexy Timms delves into the dynamics of power and love, showing how relationships can evolve from professional to personal, challenging both parties to grow and adapt. Through these stories, the genre explores the transformative power of love, suggesting that it can overcome even the most entrenched barriers of social class and personal history.

Character development is another cornerstone of the genre, with protagonists often undergoing significant personal growth as they navigate their relationships. *The Billionaire's Wake-up-call Girl* by Annika Martin is a delightful tale that combines humor with emotional depth, showing how love can serve as a catalyst for change, pushing characters to reevaluate their priorities and embrace their vulnerabilities. Martin's novel is a testament to the genre's ability to balance light-hearted romance with meaningful character arcs.

The billionaire romance genre also plays with the trope of the "Cinderella story," modernizing it to fit contemporary sensibilities and desires. *The Cinderella Deal* by Jennifer Crusie, though not strictly fitting the billionaire archetype, cleverly adapts the rags-to-riches romance, demonstrating the genre's flexibility and ability to inspire and uplift through stories of love transcending societal and economic barriers. Crusie's work underscores the genre's enduring appeal and its capacity to reimagine classic narratives in fresh, engaging ways.

In recent years, the genre has expanded to include more diverse voices and stories, reflecting a broader range of experiences and backgrounds. *The Wedding Date* by Jasmine Guillory introduces readers to a contemporary romance that blends elements of the billionaire trope, focusing on diversity, representation, and modern love. Guillory's work highlights the genre's evolution, showcasing its ability to adapt and remain relevant in a changing cultural landscape.

Finally, the billionaire romance genre is notable for its active community of readers and writers who share a passion for stories that blend the allure of wealth with the universal quest for love and connection. Through online forums, book clubs, and social media, fans of the genre connect over their favorite books, authors, and tropes, fostering a vibrant community that supports and celebrates the genre's diversity and creativity. This communal aspect enriches the reading experience, allowing for a shared enjoyment of the billionaire romance's unique blend of fantasy and reality, luxury and love.

Chapter 2

Readers' Expectations

As a billionaire romance author across multiple tropes, I've learned that understanding reader expectations is not just a part of the craft—it's essential to the soul of your writing journey. You're treading a path where every word you write not only paints a picture of luxury and desire but also resonates with the hearts of those who dream alongside you. Your readers are looking for an escape, a dive into a world where love defies all odds and where wealth and power play pivotal roles in the dance of romance. They seek characters who are as complex as they are captivating and plots that weave the billionaire lifestyles with the depth of genuine emotional connection. Let's delve into these expectations with examples from the genre that not only illuminate the path but also inspire your journey.

The emotional depth and growth of your characters are paramount. Readers crave to see how love can transform the seemingly invincible billionaire, making them vulnerable and more human. Consider how, in *The Bargain* by Vanessa Waltz, the protagonist's emotional journey from a cold, hard businessman to a man capable of love and sacrifice captures readers' hearts. Your narrative should aim to peel back the layers of your billionaire character, revealing their fears, hopes, and dreams. This transformation, powered by love, becomes a beacon for readers, guiding them through the emotional landscapes you create.

Authenticity in depicting the billionaire lifestyle is critical. While the allure of private jets, exotic locations, and lavish parties is undeniable, the glimpse into the real challenges and responsibilities of wealth truly engages readers. In *Tempted by Trouble* by Susan Arden, the portrayal of the billionaire's life goes beyond surface glamor, touching on the complexities of business and personal ethics. Your story should strive to balance the fantasy of luxury with the reality of its implications, crafting a narrative that feels aspirational and grounded.

The chemistry between your protagonists is the spark that lights the fire of your story. It's not just about physical attraction but the profound connection that develops through shared struggles and triumphs. Look at how *Bared to You* by Sylvia Day explores the intense, sometimes tumultuous relationship between Eva and Gideon, their chemistry evolving with every challenge they face together. Your writing should aim to create a bond between your characters that is as believable as it is electric, drawing readers deeper into the story.

Conflict and tension are the engines of your plot. These challenges keep readers on edge, whether arising from internal doubts, external threats, or societal pressures. In *Manwhore* by Katy Evans, the tension between the characters is not just personal but also professional, adding layers to their relationship. Your story should weave these threads of conflict with care, ensuring that each obstacle feels insurmountable yet inevitably leads to growth and deeper connection.

The transformation of your billionaire protagonist under the influence of love is a journey that readers cherish. In *Stranded with a Billionaire* by Jessica Clare, the billionaire's shift from a self-centered tycoon to a caring partner showcases the transformative power of love. Your narrative should highlight this evolution, demonstrating how even the most guarded hearts can open in the face of true companionship.

A strong, independent love interest who challenges the billionaire is essential. In *The Contract* by Melanie Moreland, the love interest's strength and moral integrity challenge the billionaire to grow and confront his flaws. Your story needs to craft a partner who is not just a foil but a catalyst for change, adding depth and dynamism to the romance.

Surprises and twists in the plot captivate readers, keeping them guessing and engaged. *The Twist* by Claire Adams exemplifies how unexpected revelations can add excitement and depth to the story. Your writing should aim to incorporate twists that feel organic to the narrative, enhancing the plot and deepening the characters' development.

A satisfying conclusion ties up all narrative threads, leaving readers fulfilled. In *The Greek's Pregnant Lover* by Lucy Monroe, the comprehensive resolution provides closure not only for the central couple but also for secondary characters and subplots. Your story should strive for an ending that feels complete, offering resolution and satisfaction on all fronts.

Secondary characters enrich the narrative, providing contrast, support, and additional layers of conflict. *The Wall of Winnipeg and Me* by Mariana Zapata demonstrates how well-developed secondary characters can enhance the story's world and deepen the central relationship. Your narrative should include a cast of characters contributing to the story's richness and complexity.

Incorporating realistic challenges related to wealth and power adds depth to your story. *Dirty Filthy Rich Men* by Laurelin Paige delves into the ethical dilemmas and personal conflicts accompanying great wealth. Your writing should explore the complexities of the billionaire lifestyle, making your characters' experiences more authentic and relatable.

Finally, contemporary themes and societal issues can lend relevance and depth to your billionaire romance. *Beautiful Bastard* by Christina Lauren tackles the dynamics of power and consent within a corporate setting, making the story entertaining and reflective of broader societal concerns. Your narrative should aim to weave in themes that resonate with today's readers, making your story a source of escape and a mirror to the world.

Understanding these expectations and masterfully incorporating them into your writing will meet and exceed your readers' reading pleasures. Your journey as a bestselling billionaire romance author is not just about telling stories; it's about crafting experiences that linger, that move, and ultimately, that connect with the very essence of romance. Let others's works in this genre inspire you, guide you, and ignite your passion to write stories that will be binged.

Chapter 3

Tropes

Billionaire romance novels are beloved for their familiar yet enticing tropes that draw readers into a world of luxury, power, and passionate love. These tropes serve as the backbone of the genre, creating a framework for stories that both comfort and captivate. Let's explore some of the most prevalent ones in a billionaire romance story, each offering its unique twist on love among the ultra-wealthy.

The Reluctant Billionaire: Often, the billionaire protagonist is portrayed as someone who is burdened rather than liberated by their wealth. This trope delves into the complexities of a life filled with material abundance but lacking genuine human connections. The reluctant billionaire may see their wealth as a barrier to finding true love, fearing that others are only interested in them for their money.

The Cinderella Story: One of the most beloved tropes, this narrative features a love interest from a modest background that catches the wealthy protagonist's eye. The stark contrast between their worlds adds to the drama and allure of their romance. This trope speaks to the universal dream of being swept off one's feet into a life of unimaginable luxury and love.

The Marriage of Convenience: Here, the billionaire and their partner enter into a marriage for practical reasons—be it for business advantages, to claim an inheritance, or to maintain a certain social standing. Of course, what starts as a transactional relationship inevitably blossoms into genuine love, challenging the characters' perceptions of love and marriage.

The Secret Billionaire: In this trope, the billionaire protagonist hides their true wealth and identity, wanting to be loved for who they are and not for their bank account. The revelation of their true identity often leads to conflict and a test of trust between the couple, ultimately reinforcing the idea that love transcends material wealth.

Office Romance: The billionaire boss and their employee find themselves entangled in a romance that blurs the lines between professional and personal. This trope explores power, ambition, and attraction dynamics, setting the stage for a captivating forbidden romance.

Enemies to Lovers: Initially, the billionaire and their love interest are at odds, perhaps due to a business rivalry or a bad first impression. The tension between them slowly transforms into passionate love, proving that sometimes, love is found in the most unexpected places.

The Damaged Billionaire: This trope centers on a billionaire with a troubled past or deep emotional wounds. The love interest becomes a source of healing and understanding, showcasing the redemptive power of love and the strength required to open one's heart again.

The Protector: The billionaire takes on the role of protector, often stepping in to save the love interest from a dangerous situation or threat. This trope highlights safety, trust, and the instinct to protect those he loves, regardless of the cost.

The Second Chance Romance: Former lovers, separated by circumstances or misunderstandings, reunite and discover that their feelings for each other haven't faded. This trope is a testament to the enduring power of love and the idea that true love can overcome even the longest odds.

The Playful Bet: A wager or challenge brings together the billionaire and their love interest, sparking an initial connection that evolves into a deep romance. The playful nature of their relationship masks deeper feelings, leading to a surprise revelation of love.

The International Love Affair: The billionaire and their love interest find love while traveling or in a foreign country. This trope immerses readers in exotic locales and cultures, adding an adventurous element to the romance.

Fake Relationship: To appease family or to serve a public image, the billionaire and the love interest pretend to be in a relationship. The charade forces them to spend time together, setting the stage for real feelings to develop amidst the facade.

The Redemption Arc: A billionaire known for their ruthless behavior or playboy lifestyle undergoes a significant transformation spurred by their love for the protagonist. This trope explores themes of personal growth, forgiveness, and the impact of love on one's character.

The Secret Child: A hidden pregnancy or unknown child comes to light, reconnecting the billionaire with their love interest and introducing the stakes of family and legacy. This trope adds layers of complexity to the romance, dealing with themes of responsibility, reconciliation, and family bonds.

Forced Proximity: Due to unforeseen circumstances, the billionaire and their love interest must live or work closely together. The close quarters fuel their attraction and force them to confront their feelings, accelerating the romance in a pressure cooker of emotions and desires.

The Disguise or Secret Identity: Similar to the secret billionaire, but in this trope, one of the characters adopts a disguise or assumes a false identity. The reasons vary, from hiding from danger to investigating a suspicion, leading to intriguing scenarios where love blossoms under the guise of deception. The eventual reveal tests the couple's trust and love, adding an exciting twist to their romance.

Opposites Attract: This classic trope brings together a billionaire and a love interest from vastly different worlds or with opposing personalities. The billionaire's lavish lifestyle contrasts sharply with the love interest's more straightforward, perhaps more grounded way of life. Their differences cause friction initially but ultimately prove that love can bridge any gap, offering a story of mutual growth and understanding.

The Rescue Mission: Here, the billionaire actively works to rescue or save the love interest from a difficult situation, whether it's a kidnapping, a bad relationship, or a personal crisis. This trope emphasizes the hero's bravery and the depth of their commitment, showcasing a grand gesture of love that solidifies the couple's bond.

The Contractual Relationship: Beyond a marriage of convenience, this arrangement involves a contract or agreement that initially brings the couple together for reasons other than love, such as to appease family, fulfill a will's stipulation, or achieve a business goal. The contractual terms set the stage for a romance that develops from artificial beginnings to genuine connections.

The Secret Admirer: One character, often the billionaire, admires the other from afar, perhaps sending anonymous gifts or messages. The mystery and intrigue of the secret admirer's identity add a layer of excitement to the romance, building anticipation until the big reveal.

The Reformed Playboy: The billionaire character has a reputation as a playboy or heartbreaker but changes their ways after meeting the love interest. This trope explores themes of transformation and redemption, highlighting the impact of finding 'the one' on a person's life choices and behavior.

Amnesia: A twist filled with suspense and mystery, where the billionaire, the love interest, or both suffer from amnesia. The struggle to remember their past or their relationship adds a compelling obstacle to their romance, testing their love and commitment in unique ways as they rediscover each other.

The Love Triangle: Involving a billionaire, the love interest, and a third party, this trope adds tension and jealousy to the romance, creating a compelling conflict that tests the strength and true nature of the couple's feelings for each other. The resolution often involves difficult choices and dramatic revelations.

The Royal Romance: Elevating the stakes with titles and crowns, this trope introduces a royal character, often with obligations and duties that conflict with their ambitions for love. The blend of billionaire luxury with the allure of royalty offers a double fantasy that captivates readers with its promise of palaces, balls, and fairy-tale endings.

The Grumpy Billionaire and the Sunshine Love Interest: This trope contrasts the brooding, often cynical billionaire with a love interest full of optimism and warmth. The dynamic between these opposites brings light to the billionaire's dark world, highlighting the transformative power of love and positivity.

The Accidental Pregnancy: This trope introduces an unexpected pregnancy that brings the billionaire and the love interest closer together. Initially, the news may shock or challenge them, but as they navigate the complexities of this surprise, their relationship deepens. This trope explores themes of responsibility, family, and how an unplanned event can lead to a profound and lasting love.

The Redemption of the Villain: Occasionally, a character initially presented as the antagonist or villain in the story undergoes significant character development, revealing a softer side that redeems them in the eyes of the love interest —and the reader. This transformation often occurs due to the love and influence of the main character, showcasing the power of love to change even the hardest hearts.

The Childhood Sweethearts: Reuniting after years apart, the billionaire and their first love rediscover each other, rekindling a romance that was never truly forgotten. This trope plays on the nostalgia and depth of a shared past, emphasizing that true love can withstand time and distance.

The Fake Engagement: Similar to the fake relationship, this trope specifically involves a pretend engagement, often to make someone else jealous, to secure a business deal, or to appease family expectations. The public nature of an engagement adds an extra layer of complication and scrutiny, heightening the tension and eventual realization of true feelings.

The Billionaire with a Cause: Here, the billionaire is deeply involved in philanthropy or a personal mission, showing a compassionate and selfless side that endears them to the love interest. This trope highlights the idea that wealth can be a force for good and that true fulfillment comes from giving back.

The Bodyguard Romance: The billionaire falls for their protector, a bodyguard hired to keep them safe from imminent threats. This setup creates an intimate, high-stakes environment where proximity and mutual respect kindle a forbidden attraction, exploring themes of loyalty, duty, and the crossing of professional boundaries.

The Hidden Heir: A secret child or heir is revealed, adding unexpected responsibilities and changing the billionaire's perspective on life and love. This trope introduces elements of surprise and responsibility, challenging the billionaire to grow and embrace new roles for the sake of family and love.

The Beauty and the Beast: Drawing inspiration from the classic fairy tale, this trope features a billionaire who is gruff, scarred, or otherwise "beastly" in demeanor or appearance, softened by the love and kindness of the "beauty." It's a tale of looking beyond the surface to find true love, emphasizing inner beauty and the transformative power of love.

The Rags to Riches Story: In a twist on the Cinderella story, the love interest not only enters the billionaire's world but also rises to their success and wealth, with or without the billionaire's help. This self-made journey highlights themes of ambition, independence, and the realization that love and success are not mutually exclusive.

The Secret Life: One character leads a secret life, whether as a spy, a vigilante, or living under a false identity for safety reasons. Their double life creates a barrier to intimacy that can only be overcome by trust and love, adding suspense and intrigue to the romance.

The Arranged Marriage: Unlike a marriage of convenience, this trope involves families or societies that arrange the marriage between the billionaire and the love interest for cultural, political, or financial reasons. The couple must find their way from fulfilling familial obligations to developing authentic feelings, exploring themes of autonomy, tradition, and the unexpected paths to love.

The Forced Marriage: Unlike a marriage of convenience entered willingly by both parties, the forced marriage trope involves characters who are compelled by external pressures —be it family, financial, or societal—to marry. The journey from resentment or indifference to love and mutual respect under such constrained beginnings provides a rich narrative full of potential growth and deep emotional connections.

Chapter 4

Key Elements in a Billionaire Romance

Understanding the elements of a billionaire romance novel is key to creating a story that resonates with readers and stands out in a crowded market. These novels, famous for their blend of romance and high society, rely on several core components to capture the reader's imagination and heart. Let's break down these essential elements, ensuring your path to writing a compelling billionaire romance novel is clear and straightforward.

First and foremost, the billionaire protagonist is a central figure in these stories. This character often embodies power, success, and the kind of lifestyle most people only dream about. However, adding depth to this character beyond their wealth is crucial. Readers look for a complex personality, hidden vulnerabilities, and a backstory that explains their motivations and fears. For example, in *Bared to You* by

Sylvia Day, the billionaire Gideon Cross is portrayed not just as wealthy and powerful but also as a man with a troubled past, which makes him more relatable and intriguing.

The love interest in these novels often provides a contrast to the billionaire's world. This character doesn't necessarily need to come from a different economic background, but they should bring a new perspective or challenge to the billionaire's life. Their strength, independence, and moral compass are essential traits that attract the billionaire and engage the reader. *The Contract* by Melanie Moreland is an excellent example, where the love interest, Avery, challenges the protagonist, Richard, forcing him to see the world and his actions in a new light.

A compelling plot is what keeps readers turning the pages. While the romance between the billionaire and their love interest is central, incorporating obstacles, misunderstandings, and external pressures adds excitement and depth to the story. These challenges should test the couple's relationship, providing opportunities for growth and proving their love is strong enough to overcome adversity. In *The Price of Scandal* by Lucy Score, the plot weaves corporate intrigue and personal demons, creating a rich narrative that engages the reader.

The setting plays a significant role in billionaire romance novels. Luxurious homes, exotic travel destinations, and high-stakes business environments are more than just backdrops; they are integral to the story, reflecting the billionaire's lifestyle and influencing the plot's development. The vivid depiction of these settings helps transport readers into a world of luxury and drama. *Lothaire* by Kresley Cole, for example, immerses readers in a variety of richly described settings that enhance the supernatural and high-stakes elements of the romance.

Emotional depth is what truly connects readers to the characters and their journey. A billionaire romance novel must explore its characters' emotional challenges and growth, making their journey to love believable and rewarding. The story should delve into their fears, desires, and the obstacles they face in opening their hearts to each other. *The Billionaire's Wake-up-call Girl* by Annika Martin demonstrates this beautifully, blending humor with deep emotional development.

Steamy scenes often feature in billionaire romance novels, adding to the intensity of the romantic connection between characters. These scenes should complement the emotional development of the relationship rather than overshadow it and be crafted with care to enhance the story's overall impact. *Release Me* by J. Kenner balances steamy scenes and emotional depth, enriching the characters' connection.

Secondary characters and subplots can add layers to the narrative, providing additional conflict, humor, or support for the main storyline. Well-developed secondary characters can enrich the novel's world and offer further insights into the protagonist's personality. *Wallbanger* by Alice Clayton is notable for its memorable secondary characters who contribute significantly to the story's humor and emotional landscape.

Finally, a satisfying conclusion is essential in a billionaire romance novel. The ending should resolve the central conflict and provide the couple with a believable happily ever after (HEA). This resolution doesn't have to be predictable but should leave readers feeling content and hopeful for the characters' future together. *Manwhore* by Katy Evans delivers a conclusion that not only satisfies the buildup of romantic tension but also ties up the story's loose ends in a believable and fulfilling way.

Each element is crucial in creating a billionaire romance novel that captivates and satisfies readers. By focusing on these key components, you can write a story that stands out for its compelling characters, engaging plot, and emotional depth, all set against a backdrop of luxury and power.

Chapter 5

Building your Believable Billionaire

Building a believable billionaire romance requires more than just lavish settings and grand gestures of love. It demands a deep understanding of what makes relationships work in the context of extreme wealth and power differentials. The first step is creating multi-dimensional characters. Billionaires in these stories should have their own set of challenges, vulnerabilities, and growth arcs. They are not just their bank accounts; they have pasts, fears, dreams, and flaws that make them relatable to readers. The complexity of these characters is what draws readers in and makes them invest in the romance.

The love interest is equally important in grounding the billionaire romance in believability. This character often contrasts the billionaire's world, bringing their own strengths, challenges, and perspective. They should not be mere accessories to the billionaire's life but have their own goals, independence, and agency. Their interactions with the billionaire should spark growth and change in both characters, making their eventual union desirable, earned, and believable.

The development of the romantic relationship is central to making a billionaire romance believable. The connection between the characters should evolve naturally, with a mix of chemistry, conflict, and companionship driving their story. It's essential to show why these two individuals, despite their differences in wealth and lifestyle, are drawn to each other and how they complement and challenge each other. This emotional depth ensures the relationship feels real and sustainable beyond the initial spark of attraction.

Incorporating realistic conflicts arising from the billionaire lifestyle can add believability to the romance. Issues such as media scrutiny, privacy concerns, and the pressures of public life can create obstacles for the couple. These challenges can test the strength of their relationship, providing opportunities for character development and deeper bonding. The resolution of these conflicts can reinforce the story's emotional core and highlight the couple's commitment to each other.

The setting and backdrop of the story play a significant role in creating a believable billionaire romance. While luxurious lifestyles and exotic locations are staples of the genre, their portrayal needs to be grounded in reality. Descriptions of settings and lifestyles should be detailed and well-researched, allowing readers to immerse themselves in the world of the story while still feeling authentic. This authenticity helps readers suspend disbelief and fully engage with the romantic journey.

Supporting characters can add depth and believability to the billionaire romance. Friends, family, and even rivals of the main characters can provide insights into their personalities and values and contribute to the plot's development. These characters should have their own distinct voices and roles within the story, enriching the narrative and reinforcing the believability of the romance.

Dialogue is a crucial element in building a believable billionaire romance. The way characters speak to each other should reflect their backgrounds, personalities, and emotional states. Authentic, engaging dialogue can reveal character dynamics, build tension, and advance the romantic plot in a way that feels natural and true to life. Effective dialogue captures the essence of the characters' relationship, convincing the reader of their interactions and growing connection.

The pacing of the romance is another factor in its believability. The relationship should not feel rushed or forced; instead, it should unfold at a pace that allows genuine emotional development. Slow-building romance, where characters gradually reveal themselves to each other and overcome obstacles together, often feels more realistic and satisfying. This measured approach ensures that when milestones in the relationship are reached, they feel earned and impactful.

Emotional realism is key to making a billionaire romance believable. The characters' feelings—the initial attraction, the deepening of their connection, or struggles—should be portrayed with depth and fine detail. The emotional journey should resonate with readers, reflecting real-life experiences of love, doubt, fear, and joy. The story becomes more relatable and engaging by grounding the romance in genuine emotions.

Incorporating external challenges related to the billionaire's world can enhance the believability of the romance. These might include business pressures, ethical dilemmas, or conflicts with family expectations. How these challenges impact the relationship and how the couple navigates them can add a layer of complexity and realism to the story. It shows that love involves compromise, sacrifice, and teamwork, even in the most glamorous settings.

The resolution of the romance should feel satisfying and realistic within the story's context. A believable billionaire romance doesn't necessarily require a fairy-tale ending, but the conclusion should be consistent with the characters' growth and the story's themes. Whether it's a happily-ever-after (HEA) or a happy-for-now (HFN), the ending should reflect the characters' journey and the obstacles they've overcome together.

Finally, research and authenticity in depicting the billionaire lifestyle are crucial for believability. This includes understanding the things associated with wealth, the responsibilities and challenges it brings, and how it affects relationships. By weaving in authentic details and showing a deep understanding of this lifestyle, the story not only gains depth but also becomes more engaging and believable to readers fascinated by the world of the ultra-wealthy.

Chapter 6

Crafting your Billionaire Protagonist

Crafting the billionaire protagonist in your romance novel requires a thoughtful approach to ensure they are both aspirational and relatable. Start by delving into their backstory, considering how their wealth was acquired and the impact it has had on their personality and worldview. It's important to remember that your protagonist should be more than just their bank account; they need depth and complexity to be genuinely compelling. Consider their challenges on their journey to success and how these experiences have shaped their character. This will help you create a well-rounded billionaire with whom readers can connect personally.

Your billionaire protagonist should possess a unique blend of strengths and vulnerabilities. While their wealth affords them power and confidence, revealing their insecurities or fears makes them human and relatable. Perhaps they struggle with trust issues due to past betrayals or carry the weight of loneliness at the top. By showcasing these vulnerabilities, you invite readers to see the person behind the wealth, making your protagonist more engaging and multi-dimensional.

Give your billionaire a cause or passion beyond their business ventures. This adds depth to their character and provides opportunities for them to interact with the world meaningfully. Whether it's philanthropy, environmental conservation, or a creative pursuit, this passion can serve as a catalyst for growth and change, both in themselves and in their relationships. It also offers a glimpse into their values and what they hold dear, further endearing them to readers.

A compelling billionaire protagonist is not defined solely by their success but by how they handle failure and adversity. Show moments where they face setbacks or make mistakes, and more importantly, how they respond to these challenges. Do they rise with resilience, or do they need to learn humility? These trials are essential for character development, allowing readers to witness their journey of self-discovery and transformation, making the protagonist's journey more engaging.

Incorporate a sense of mystery or intrigue around your billionaire protagonist. Perhaps there's a secret in their past or an aspect of their life they keep closely guarded. This not only adds layers to your character but also drives the plot forward, as the love interest and the reader alike are drawn into uncovering the truth. A well-crafted mystery can keep readers hooked and eager to learn more about the protagonist's true self.

Your billionaire protagonist should also possess a sharp intellect and a knack for innovation. Their wealth should be a testament to their creativity, determination, and ability to think outside the box. This intelligence can be a sexy and attractive trait, drawing the love interest and the reader alike. It also allows for exciting plot developments, as their business acumen can play a crucial role in overcoming obstacles within the story.

Consider giving your billionaire protagonist a philanthropic side. This humanizes them and provides a platform to showcase their values and beliefs. Philanthropy can be a means of redemption for a flawed character or a way to challenge their worldview and spur personal growth. It's a powerful tool for demonstrating the protagonist's capacity for kindness and empathy, qualities that make them more appealing to the reader.

A touch of vulnerability goes a long way in making your billionaire protagonist relatable. Perhaps they have a personal loss they've never fully recovered from, or they're grappling with the fear of never finding true love. These vulnerabilities make the character more human, fostering a deeper connection with the reader. They also offer opportunities for emotional growth and development throughout the story.

Ensure your billionaire protagonist experiences genuine growth throughout the novel. Their journey should not only be about finding love but also about personal transformation. This could involve learning to open up emotionally, reassessing their priorities in life, or overcoming a personal demon. Readers should feel that the protagonist is a better person by the end of the story, thanks to the trials they've faced and the love they've found.

Balance is key when depicting the lifestyle of your billionaire protagonist. While it's important to include elements of luxury and extravagance inherent to their status, these should not overshadow the personal and emotional aspects of the story. The focus on lavish settings and possessions should serve to enhance the narrative, not detract from the emotional depth and development of the character.

Your protagonist should also display a strong sense of loyalty and integrity. Despite their wealth and the power that comes with it, they remain true to their word and committed to those they care about. This integrity wins the respect of other characters and the reader alike, establishing the billionaire as a hero worthy of admiration and love.

Incorporate moments of humor and light-heartedness in your billionaire's personality. No one is always serious, and these moments can make your protagonist more likable and relatable. A well-timed joke or playful banter with the love interest can add a much-needed pause in a tension-filled narrative, endearing your billionaire to readers even more.

Finally, remember that your billionaire protagonist should actively contribute to their love story. They shouldn't just be objects of desire based on wealth and status but a dynamic character who pursues their love interest with intention and vulnerability. Their actions should demonstrate their willingness to risk their heart for love, proving they are not just wealthy figureheads but a passionate individual capable of deep emotional connections.

By focusing on these aspects, you'll be able to write a billionaire protagonist who is compelling and multifaceted, and someone readers can root for and fall in love with throughout your novel. Balancing their wealth and power with genuine emotion, vulnerability, and growth is key to creating a memorable character that stands out in the billionaire romance genre.

Chapter 7

The Role of Conflict

In the confines of a billionaire romance story, conflict serves as the crucible through which characters are forged, relationships are tested, and true love is ultimately revealed. It is not merely an obstacle to be overcome but a vital element that adds depth, tension, and realism to the narrative. Conflict in billionaire romance often arises from the clash of worlds—the luxurious yet isolating bubble of wealth and power meets the grounded, frequently simpler life of the love interest. This intersection creates a fertile ground for exploring themes of trust, sacrifice, and the universal quest for connection beyond material wealth. Through these trials, characters are pushed to grow, confront their fears and biases, and fight for a love that transcends societal boundaries and personal limitations.

The conflict between personal desires and professional obligations is common in billionaire romances. The protagonist, often trapped in the demands of their empire, must navigate the treacherous waters of corporate intrigue, family expectations, and the pursuit of personal happiness. This tension highlights the sacrifices and compromises inherent in a life of wealth, challenging the billionaire to prioritize their heart's desires over their business empire. Through this struggle, the character's depth and capacity for love are revealed, making their journey toward happiness all the more rewarding and believable to the reader.

External conflicts, such as familial disapproval or societal scrutiny, add another layer of complexity to the romance. These challenges test the couple's commitment and force them to confront the realities of their relationship in the public eye. In stories like these, love is not just a private affair but a public spectacle, subject to the opinions and judgments of others. The couple must navigate these pressures, proving that their love is genuine and strong enough to withstand external forces. This battle against societal norms and expectations underscores the transformative power of love to overcome obstacles.

Secrets and misunderstandings are potent sources of conflict in billionaire romances, weaving suspense and intrigue into the fabric of the relationship. Whether it's a hidden past, a misunderstood intention, or a secret that threatens to unravel the trust between the characters, these elements keep readers hooked, eager to see how the truth will come to light. The resolution of these secrets often serves as a turning point in the relationship, a moment of vulnerability and honesty that deepens the connection between the characters and propels the narrative toward its climax.

The internal conflict within the billionaire character themselves often serves as a compelling focal point. Burdened by their wealth and what it represents, they struggle with feelings of isolation, unworthiness, or the fear that love cannot be untangled from their fortune. This introspective battle challenges the billionaire to confront their own demons and redefine their understanding of love and happiness beyond the metrics of success and failure. It's a journey of self-discovery that enriches the romance, making the eventual union not just a merger of hearts but a healing of souls.

In billionaire romances, the disparity in social or economic status between the protagonists can be a significant source of conflict. This difference often brings to light issues of power dynamics, pride, and prejudice, challenging both characters to look beyond the surface and appreciate the intrinsic worth of the other. The journey towards understanding and acceptance is fraught with challenges, but precisely, these hurdles make the romance all the more compelling and the characters' growth more pronounced.

The trope of rivals turned lovers is a testament to the role of conflict in creating dynamic and engaging billionaire romances. Here, competition and ambition initially drive the protagonists apart, only for them to discover a mutual respect and attraction that complicates their rivalry. This evolution from adversaries to allies to lovers is a thrilling journey that underscores the idea that love can flourish in the most unexpected places, transforming enmity into the most profound form of partnership.

Conflict also serves to highlight the theme of sacrifice. Characters often face difficult choices that test their values and commitment to one another. Whether it's giving up a cherished dream, stepping away from a family business, or risking social ostracization, these moments of sacrifice underscore the depth of the characters' love and commitment, elevating the romance from a simple love story to a testament to the power of love to inspire change.

The resolution of conflict in billionaire romances is a pivotal moment that brings closure to the narrative and reaffirms the story's themes. It's where the characters' journey through adversity culminates in a deeper understanding and appreciation of one another. How conflicts are resolved can vary—from grand gestures that demonstrate love and commitment to quiet moments of insight and forgiveness—but the key is that these resolutions feel earned and genuine to the characters' development.

The role of conflict in the billionaire romance genre underscores the genre's broader exploration of love as a force capable of bridging divides, healing wounds, and transforming lives. Through the trials and tribulations faced by the characters, readers are reminded of the resilience of the human heart and the enduring power of love. In crafting these tales of passion, conflict, and redemption, authors entertain and offer hope and inspiration, affirming the belief that love, in all its forms, is indeed the greatest luxury.

Chapter 8

Avoiding Cliches & Creating Depth

When writing your billionaire romance novel, steering clear of clichés and infusing your narrative with depth are crucial steps to ensure your story resonates with readers. Clichés, while familiar, can often feel tired and predictable, leading to a lack of engagement from your audience. To avoid this, focus on originality in your plot and character development. Start by examining common tropes within the genre and think about how you can twist them to surprise your readers. This doesn't mean you have to reinvent the wheel completely, but consider approaching a familiar scenario from a new angle or with an unexpected outcome.

Creating depth in your characters is essential for moving beyond stereotypes. Your billionaire protagonist shouldn't just be a cardboard cutout of wealth and power; they need layers and feelings that make them feel real. Dive into their past experiences, fears, dreams, and the motivations behind their actions. What drives them beyond the accumulation of wealth? Fleshing out their backstory and personality will help you avoid the cliché of the superficial billionaire and instead present a character with whom readers can empathize and connect.

Dialogue plays a significant role in avoiding clichés and adding depth to your story. Resist the temptation to rely on overused phrases or exchanges that don't add to character development. Each conversation should reveal something about the characters or advance the plot meaningfully. Use dialogue to showcase your characters' unique voices, including their intellect, humor, and vulnerabilities. This will make your characters more distinct and your narrative more engaging.

The setting of your billionaire romance can easily fall into the cliché trap of lavish lifestyles and exotic locales. While these elements can be a fun aspect of the genre, adding depth requires you to do more than just describe lavish settings. Show how these environments affect your characters or reflect their internal states. Perhaps the cold, minimalist design of the billionaire's mansion mirrors their emotional isolation. Tying the setting to character development makes your story more immersive and meaningful.

In developing the romance at the heart of your novel, avoid the cliché of instant love or unfounded attraction. Build the relationship gradually, allowing readers to see why the characters are drawn to each other beyond physical appearance or wealth. Highlight shared interests, emotional connections, and moments of vulnerability that bring them closer together. This slow build-up makes their eventual union more believable and satisfying, enriching the narrative with depth and realism.

Conflict is a key element in any romance novel, but relying on misunderstandings that could be solved with a simple conversation is a common cliché. Instead, introduce conflicts that stem from the characters' backgrounds, personal flaws, or external pressures. These challenges should require genuine effort and growth, making the resolution more rewarding. This approach avoids clichés and adds complexity to the story and its characters.

Character flaws are another area where you can add depth and avoid clichés. Your billionaire protagonist shouldn't be perfect; their flaws make them human and relatable. However, avoid the cliché of the "damaged" billionaire whose only flaw is a troubled past. Consider more in-depth imperfections, such as fear of commitment due to personal ambition or difficulty expressing emotions. These traits offer more opportunities for character growth and development throughout the story.

The supporting cast in your novel can easily become clichéd if they only serve as plot devices or one-dimensional foils to the main characters. Give them goals, motivations, and arcs that intersect with or contrast the main narrative. This adds depth to the overall story and creates a richer, more believable world. Characters should feel like they exist beyond their interactions with the protagonists, making your story more engaging and complex.

In crafting your novel's plot, challenge the predictability often found in romance narratives. While readers expect a happily ever after, the journey there shouldn't be straightforward. Introduce twists, turns, and obstacles unique to your story and characters. By weaving a plot that keeps readers guessing, you enhance the depth of your narrative and hold their interest from start to finish.

Your characters' emotional journey is a crucial element in creating depth. Beyond the surface-level attraction and romantic gestures, delve into the emotional growth that occurs as they navigate their relationship. This journey should be fraught with self-discovery, compromises, and moments of introspection. By focusing on the emotional development of your characters, you create a more compelling and heartfelt story that transcends clichéd romance.

Incorporating themes that resonate on a deeper level can also help you avoid clichés and add depth to your billionaire romance novel. Themes such as the search for identity, the impact of wealth on personal relationships, or the struggle for work-life balance can lend your story a layer of complexity beyond the typical romance plot. These themes can challenge your characters and readers, making your novel more thought-provoking and memorable.

Lastly, your narrative voice and style play a significant role in avoiding clichés and creating depth. Choose a voice that complements your story's tone and reflects your characters' personalities. A unique narrative style can set your story apart and freshly engage readers. Experiment with different perspectives or storytelling techniques that best serve your narrative, ensuring that your approach enhances the depth and originality of your billionaire romance novel.

Focusing on these aspects ensures that your billionaire romance novel stands out for its originality, depth, and engaging storytelling. Avoiding clichés isn't just about steering clear of specific plot points or character types; it's about approaching your narrative with creativity and thoughtfulness. With these strategies, you're well on your way to writing a billionaire romance that captures readers' hearts and leaves a lasting impression.

Chapter 9

Balancing Power & Vulnerability

In your journey to craft a captivating billionaire romance novel, one of the most intricate dances you'll choreograph is between power and vulnerability. Your billionaire protagonist, swathed in wealth and influence, naturally exudes an aura of power. This power is multifaceted, emanating from their financial resources, social status, and, often, their sheer will to succeed. Yet, for your story to resonate deeply, you must peel back the layers of this power to reveal the vulnerability hidden beneath. In these moments of vulnerability, your character becomes relatable, transforming from a distant figure of fantasy into a living, breathing person with whom readers can connect.

Balancing this power with vulnerability begins with understanding your character's backstory. Every empire has its foundations; your billionaire's empire is no exception.

Delve into their past to uncover the struggles, failures, and sacrifices that paved their road to success. These historical vulnerabilities not only humanize your protagonist but also offer a contrast to their present power. It's important to weave these elements into your narrative, allowing readers glimpses of the person behind the power, someone who has faced adversity and emerged stronger, yet not unscathed.

When introducing the love interest, you find a direct path to exposing your protagonist's vulnerability. This character should challenge the billionaire in ways that money and influence can't mitigate. It could be through emotional connections that breach the walls your protagonist has built around their heart or through situations where wealth is irrelevant. This dynamic shifts the power balance, emphasizing that vulnerability is an equalizer in matters of the heart. Crafting scenes where the billionaire must navigate emotional landscapes without their usual tools of power fosters a deep sense of empathy and connection from your readers.

Incorporating scenes that strip your protagonist of their usual control can further highlight this balance. Imagine situations where their wealth cannot fix the problem at hand, whether it's a personal dilemma of the love interest or a challenge that requires emotional rather than financial solutions. These scenarios showcase the limitations of power and force your protagonist to confront their vulnerabilities, offering a richer, more detailed character development arc.

Dialogue is a powerful tool in revealing vulnerability. Through conversations, especially those laced with emotional stakes, you allow your billionaire to express doubts, fears, and desires openly. These exchanges can be particularly revealing when the billionaire faces situations that money can't solve, pushing them to verbalize feelings they might usually keep hidden. Crafting genuine and raw dialogue can bridge the gap between the reader and your protagonist, making the moments of vulnerability as impactful as displays of power.

The relationship dynamics in your story offer a fertile ground for exploring the interplay between power and vulnerability. Romantic developments show how the billionaire's usual dominance is challenged, not just by the love interest but by their emotional responses to them. This doesn't diminish their power but adds a layer of complexity, illustrating that true strength lies in the ability to be vulnerable with someone else. Let these dynamics evolve naturally, reflecting the gradual shifts in power as the relationship deepens.

Your protagonist's internal monologue provides a direct window into their vulnerabilities. Use it to reveal the thoughts and fears behind their confident exterior. This narrative technique allows readers to connect intimately with the billionaire, understanding their insecurities and the weight of their expectations. It humanizes your character, balancing their outer world of power with an inner world filled with doubts and desires.

The external conflicts your billionaire faces should also challenge their power and expose their vulnerabilities. Perhaps their empire is threatened, or they must navigate a world where their wealth offers no advantage. These conflicts test their resilience and force them to confront their limitations, highlighting the precarious nature of power and the universal experience of vulnerability.

Vulnerability in your protagonist can also be explored through their philanthropic efforts or causes they're passionate about. These endeavors often stem from personal experiences or losses as a conduit for showing a softer side. Engaging with these causes exposes them to emotional risks, further balancing their character between power and vulnerability.

In moments of crisis or emotional turmoil, allow your protagonist to lean on others, including the love interest or supporting characters. This reliance on others, a departure from their usual self-sufficiency, underscores their vulnerability and fosters deeper connections with those around them. It's a reminder that true power often lies in asking for help and trusting others.

Crafting a backstory that includes significant loss or failure for your billionaire protagonist not only adds depth to their character but also constantly reminds them of their vulnerability. This loss, whether it's personal or professional, influences their actions and decisions, making them more cautious or driving them to prove themselves. It's a vulnerability that shapes their identity, adding a layer of complexity to their character.

As your billionaire navigates their world, the façade of power they present to the outside world should occasionally slip, revealing their true self to the reader and the love interest. These intentional or accidental moments are pivotal in developing a multi-dimensional character. They demonstrate that beneath the veneer of control and authority lies a person with fears, hopes, and dreams.

The climax of your story should be a turning point where the billionaire fully embraces their vulnerability, recognizing it not as a weakness but as a strength. This epiphany often comes with high emotional stakes, where the protagonist must expose their true self to achieve their goals or save their relationship. It's a moment of catharsis, both for the character and the reader, reinforcing the idea that vulnerability is integral to personal growth and true love.

Finally, the resolution of your novel should reflect a new equilibrium between power and vulnerability within your billionaire protagonist. They emerge from their journey not diminished but enriched by their experiences, wielding their power with a newfound appreciation for the strength found in vulnerability. This balance makes for a satisfying end to your story and leaves your readers with a lasting impression of a character who is authentically human, relatable, and, ultimately, more lovable.

Balancing power and vulnerability in your billionaire romance novel enriches your narrative, making your characters more compelling and relatable. This equilibrium resonates with readers, drawing them into the world you've created and keeping them engaged from the first page to the last. By exploring the complexities of your protagonist's character, you craft a story that speaks to the heart of the human experience, where power and vulnerability coexist as two sides of the same coin.

Chapter 10

Complimenting the Billionaire

Creating a love interest that complements your billionaire protagonist is crucial in crafting a compelling billionaire romance novel. This character must embody qualities that not only attract the billionaire but also challenge and inspire them to grow. They must bring their own strengths to the relationship, creating a dynamic where both characters are enriched by their connection. The love interest should have a clear, strong sense of self, independent of the billionaire's world, making them an equal partner in the narrative. Their relatability to readers through their struggles, aspirations, and values adds depth to the story, fostering a connection that elevates the romance beyond mere fantasy. Creating a love interest with a compelling backstory, personal ambitions, and the courage to stand up to the billionaire ensures an engaging and believable dynamic.

The importance of making the love interest relatable cannot be overstated. They should embody qualities and face challenges that resonate with readers' experiences or aspirations. This doesn't mean they must come from a modest background, but their struggles and triumphs should be grounded in reality. You underscore their independence and strength by giving them goals and challenges outside of their relationship with the billionaire. This makes them a more compelling character and enriches the romance, as readers see a genuine partnership form based on mutual respect and admiration. A love interest who can navigate the world with or without the billionaire offers a refreshing and inspiring counterpoint to the often larger-than-life protagonist.

The dynamic between the billionaire and their love interest should be one of mutual growth. While the billionaire often undergoes a significant transformation throughout the story, it's important that the love interest also experiences growth. This could be in the form of achieving personal goals, overcoming fears, or learning to trust. Their relationship should serve as a catalyst for this development, highlighting how they complement and challenge each other. A love interest who remains static while the billionaire changes diminishes the potential for a deeply satisfying and balanced relationship. Instead, aim for a partnership where both characters evolve, reflecting the transformative power of love.

Strength is a key characteristic of a compelling love interest. This strength can manifest in various ways: emotional resilience, moral courage, or intellectual prowess. This strength allows them to match the dynamic of the billionaire, ensuring they don't become overshadowed in the narrative. For instance, a love interest who is a successful entrepreneur in their own right or passionately committed to a cause showcases a form of strength that can intrigue and attract the billionaire. By positioning the love interest as someone who can stand toe-to-toe with the billionaire, you create a relationship that is captivating and grounded in equality.

The love interest's relatability is enhanced when they navigate relatable dilemmas or confront societal issues. Perhaps they're grappling with career challenges, facing discrimination, or balancing personal aspirations with familial responsibilities. These struggles humanize the character and offer opportunities for the billionaire to support and learn from them, further deepening their bond. A love interest who actively works towards resolutions, with or without the billionaire's assistance, reinforces their role as a strong, independent character within the story.

Including a unique or quirky trait can make the love interest more memorable and endearing to readers. This could be a hobby, a passion for a particular cause, or a distinctive sense of humor. Such traits provide depth to the character, making them stand out and adding layers to the romance. These unique attributes can also serve as points of connection or contention between the characters, driving the plot and enriching their interactions. For instance, a love interest who collects vintage books might inspire a billionaire with no interest in literature to explore new worlds through reading, symbolizing their influence on each other's lives.

The love interest's ability to challenge the billionaire is crucial for creating a dynamic relationship. They should be confident in calling out the billionaire on their faults and pushing them towards personal growth. This challenging dynamic fosters respect and admiration, qualities essential for a deep and lasting love. Through these confrontations, the billionaire often experiences the most significant growth, coming to appreciate qualities they might have overlooked or undervalued before meeting their love interest.

Empathy and emotional intelligence can greatly enhance the love interest's character. These traits allow them to understand and connect with the billionaire on a deeper level, recognizing the vulnerabilities hidden behind a façade of power and confidence. An empathetic love interest can help navigate the complexities of the billionaire's world, offering support and understanding that fosters a genuine connection. This emotional depth ensures the relationship is built on more than physical attraction or superficial bonds.

The love interest's backstory plays a significant role in shaping their character. A well-developed history of triumphs, failures, and growth enriches their persona. This backstory provides context for their motivations, fears, and desires, making their actions and reactions within the story more believable and impactful. For instance, a love interest who has overcome adversity to achieve their goals brings resilience and determination that can inspire both the billionaire and the readers.

A sense of humor can be a powerful tool in making the love interest more relatable and appealing. Laughter and light-hearted moments can bridge the gap between worlds, humanizing the billionaire and grounding their romance in reality. A love interest who can make the billionaire laugh, especially in moments of tension or seriousness, adds a refreshing dynamic to the story, highlighting the joy and companionship that form the foundation of their relationship.

Creating a love interest that complements the billionaire also means designing someone who can share in their world without being consumed by it. They should have the confidence and self-assurance to navigate high society events and business dealings yet remain grounded in their values and identity. This balance ensures that the love interest remains a strong, independent character, even as they become part of the billionaire's glamorous lifestyle.

Intellectual compatibility is another aspect that should not be overlooked. A love interest who can match or challenge the billionaire in terms of intellect offers a stimulating partnership that goes beyond physical attraction. Whether through spirited debates, shared interests in specific subjects, or collaborative projects, showcasing their intellectual bond strengthens the foundation of their relationship, making it more compelling and realistic.

The love interest's interaction with secondary characters can further highlight their strength and relatability. Through friendships, familial relationships, or professional connections, you can demonstrate their ability to impact and enrich the lives of others. These interactions also offer additional perspectives on the love interest, reinforcing their role as a complex and engaging character within the narrative.

The love interest should embody qualities and desires that the billionaire admires, which they perhaps feel are missing in their lives. Whether it's a connection to family, a passion for adventure, or a commitment to philanthropy, these attributes draw the billionaire to the love interest, compelling them to pursue a relationship. By ensuring that the love interest represents an ideal or fulfills a need for the billionaire, you create a powerful dynamic where both characters are essential to each other's happiness and growth.

In creating a love interest that complements your billionaire protagonist, you are tasked with designing a character who is strong, relatable, and dynamic. They must stand as equals in the relationship, challenging and supporting the billionaire equally. By carefully considering their traits, backstory, and growth throughout the story, you can craft a love interest that enriches the narrative and captivates your readers, making your billionaire romance novel a memorable and engaging read.

Chapter 11

Dynamics of Attraction & Conflict

In the intricate dance of writing a billionaire romance novel, the dynamics of attraction and conflict serve as the heartbeat of your story. These elements are not just about creating sparks or tension; they're about delving into the complexities that make relationships feel real and compelling. Attraction goes beyond physical appeal, weaving in the intellectual, emotional, and sometimes even the adversarial aspects that draw two people together. It's the shared laughs, the heated debates, and the moments of vulnerability that deepen the connection between your characters. For example, in *"Pride and Prejudice"* by Jane Austen, Elizabeth Bennet and Mr. Darcy's attraction is fueled by their wit, pride, and prejudices, showcasing how attraction can evolve from initial misconceptions to deep understanding and love.

Conflict, on the other hand, tests the strength and depth of this attraction. It's not merely about creating obstacles for the sake of drama; it's about presenting challenges that are authentic to the characters' experiences and growth. Conflicts can stem from internal struggles, such as fears of vulnerability or commitment, or from external pressures, like societal expectations or familial obligations. In *"The Hating Game"* by Sally Thorne, Lucy and Joshua's workplace rivalry and personal insecurities fuel both their conflict and their attraction, demonstrating how closely intertwined these dynamics can be.

To create believable attraction, focus on building a connection that acknowledges the individuality of each character. Your billionaire protagonist and their love interest should be drawn to each other for reasons that transcend surface-level beauty or wealth. Perhaps it's the love interest's passion for a cause that ignites the billionaire's admiration, or the billionaire's unexpected kindness that warms the love interest's heart. These moments of genuine connection make the attraction feel more authentic and grounded.

Conflict should similarly arise from the core of who your characters are and what they value. When designing conflicts, consider how the billionaire's lifestyle could intimidate, challenge, or even alienate the love interest, and vice versa. For instance, in *"Me Before You"* by Jojo Moyes, Louisa's ordinary life and Will's disability and wealth create a complex web of personal and ethical conflicts that test their feelings for each other. This type of conflict enriches the narrative, adding layers to the romance.

The push and pull between attraction and conflict can also drive character development. As your characters navigate their feelings and the obstacles in their path, they should grow and change. This evolution is what makes the resolution of their story satisfying. In *"Wallbanger"* by Alice Clayton, Caroline and Simon's initial annoyance with each other turns into a deep attraction as they confront their own issues with relationships and intimacy, showcasing how characters can evolve through their interactions.

Use dialogue as a tool to explore the dynamics of attraction and conflict. Through their conversations, your characters can flirt, argue, and reveal their innermost thoughts and feelings. This verbal exchange allows readers to see the complexity of the characters' relationship, offering insights into their compatibility and the issues they must overcome. Dialogue can turn a simple scene into a pivotal moment of connection or confrontation.

Setting can also play a crucial role in highlighting attraction and conflict. The environments in which your characters interact can influence their mood and behavior, whether it's a secluded beach that sparks romance or a crowded social event that exacerbates their differences. In *"Beautiful Disaster"* by Jamie McGuire, the college setting amplifies Travis and Abby's tumultuous relationship, providing a backdrop that reflects their youthful passion and the challenges they face.

The physical aspect of attraction should be balanced with emotional depth. While instant chemistry can ignite interest, it's the shared experiences and emotional support that solidify the connection. Show how your characters care for each other in moments of vulnerability, how they support each other's dreams, and how they navigate disagreements. This balance ensures that the relationship feels substantial and real.

Incorporating secondary characters can enrich the dynamics of attraction and conflict. Friends, family, and rivals can offer perspectives that challenge the protagonists' relationship or provide support during difficult times. These interactions can also introduce new conflicts or help resolve existing ones, adding complexity to the narrative.

Remember that conflict doesn't always have to be dramatic or external. Internal conflicts, such as doubts about self-worth or fears of abandonment, can be just as compelling. These struggles offer a glimpse into the characters' psyche, making their journey towards love more believable.

The resolution of conflict is a critical moment in your story. It should feel earned, with both characters demonstrating growth and compromise. The way they overcome obstacles together solidifies their bond, making their eventual union all the more rewarding. This resolution shouldn't just tie up loose ends; it should reflect the depth of their connection and the lessons learned along the way.

Attraction and conflict are not static; they evolve as your story progresses. The initial spark of attraction might deepen into love, just as early conflicts might give way to understanding and mutual respect. This evolution is what keeps readers invested in the relationship, eager to see how it will unfold.

Finally, always keep your characters at the forefront of the dynamics of attraction and conflict. Their unique personalities, backgrounds, and desires should inform how they interact with each other. By staying true to your characters, you ensure that the dance between attraction and conflict feels genuine, engaging your readers from the first page to the last.

In sum, balancing the dynamics of attraction and conflict requires a real understanding of your characters and their journey. By weaving these elements together thoughtfully, you create a billionaire romance novel that captivates with its depth, realism, and emotional resonance.

Chapter 12

World-Building

World-building in a billionaire romance novel is about crafting an immersive and believable setting that enriches the narrative and enhances the romantic journey of your characters. It involves more than just describing luxurious lifestyles or exotic locales; it's about creating a backdrop reflecting the characters' internal worlds and thematic elements. Whether your setting is a bustling metropolis known for its high-stakes business world or a secluded island that offers an escape from the public eye, each detail should contribute to the mood and tone of the story. Through meticulous world-building, you invite readers into a space that feels aspirational and authentic, where love, power, and personal growth intersect in compelling ways.

When building your world, consider the social dynamics at play within the billionaire's circle. The intricacies of high society, with its unwritten rules and expectations, provide a rich blend of conflict and character development. How your characters navigate these dynamics—whether they adhere to or rebel against societal norms—can reveal much about their personalities and values. This social setting also offers opportunities for introducing secondary characters who can either support or challenge the protagonists, adding depth and complexity to the narrative.

Economic and political factors are also essential to world-building in a billionaire romance. The source of the billionaire's wealth, whether it's tech, finance, or an inherited empire, should influence the story's setting and plot. These details can provide a backdrop for external conflicts, such as corporate rivalries or ethical dilemmas, which test the characters' morals and commitment to one another. Incorporating these elements adds realism to your world and grounds the romance in issues that resonate with contemporary readers.

The physical environment plays a crucial role in setting the stage for romance and conflict. Descriptions of the billionaire's home, office, and favorite haunts should do more than illustrate luxury; they should also reflect the character's personality and the story's emotional tone. A minimalist, architecturally significant mansion might signify the billionaire's need for control and order, while a warm, cluttered apartment could reveal the love interest's focus on comfort and personal history. These settings become arenas for interaction, conflict, and intimacy, contributing to the narrative's emotional depth.

Incorporating technology and media into your world-building can add a layer of realism and tension. How characters interact with social media, the press, and the digital world can influence their relationships and the story's plot. For instance, a scandal breaking out on social media can drive the narrative forward, while technology can facilitate communication or misunderstandings between the protagonists. This modern approach to world-building reflects the realities of living in a connected world, where privacy is scarce, and public perception can change instantly.

Cultural elements enrich the tapestry of your world, adding color and texture to the narrative. Integrating aspects of the characters' heritage, traditions, and beliefs can deepen readers' understanding and provide a more immersive reading experience. Whether it's a traditional family gathering, a high-profile charity event, or a simple, culturally significant gesture, these details can make the world of your novel feel lived-in and authentic.

The legal and ethical landscape in which your billionaire operates can offer fertile ground for conflict and plot development. Whether navigating corporate law, dealing with inheritance issues, or facing ethical dilemmas related to wealth, these challenges can test the characters' integrity and commitment to each other. This aspect of world-building adds tension to the story and prompts readers to consider the complexities of power and responsibility.

Leisure and travel are often integral to the billionaire lifestyle, providing opportunities for escape and adventure. Describing luxurious vacations, exclusive resorts, or even private jets and yachts can transport readers to glamorous settings. Still, the experiences and emotions shared during these escapes deepen the romance. These moments away from the mundane world allow characters to reveal hidden aspects of themselves, strengthening their bond and advancing their relationship.

The juxtaposition of the billionaire's world with the love interest can highlight disparities in lifestyle and values, serving as a source of attraction and conflict. This contrast underscores the differences between the characters and challenges them to find common ground. The way they bridge these worlds can drive character development and propel the narrative forward.

Your world should also reflect the themes of your story, whether it's the corrupting influence of power, the isolation of wealth, or the search for authenticity in a superficial world. You create a cohesive and resonant story by aligning the setting with the narrative's themes. The world becomes a character in its own right, shaping the protagonists' journey and reflecting their inner conflicts and desires.

In crafting your world, remember to balance detail with narrative pace. While rich descriptions can enhance the setting, they should never overshadow the plot or slow the story's momentum. Strategic details that evoke the senses and emotions are more effective than exhaustive luxury items or settings inventories. This selective approach ensures that your world-building serves the story, enhancing rather than detracting from your characters' romantic and emotional journey.

As your characters evolve, so too should your world. The settings that once comforted or impressed them might lose their luster as their values and priorities change. This dynamic approach to world-building mirrors the characters' growth, making the setting an active participant in their journey. As they find love and fulfillment, the world around them gains new meaning, reflecting the transformative power of their relationship.

Through careful and thoughtful world-building, you create a vivid and compelling backdrop for your billionaire romance novel. This setting not only enchants readers but also deepens their engagement with the story, making the characters' journey toward love and understanding all the more believable and rewarding.

Chapter 13

Structuring your Story for Maximum Impact

Structuring for maximum impact involves more than just outlining a beginning, middle, and end. It requires thoughtful consideration of pacing, character development, and how each scene contributes to the overarching narrative. One practical approach is to start with a hook that immediately grabs the reader's attention. Consider *"The Night Circus"* by Erin Morgenstern, where the mysterious and magical setting is introduced right from the start, instantly pulling readers into its world. Your billionaire romance could begin with a dramatic encounter or a revealing moment, setting the tone for the romance and conflicts. This initial hook is crucial for setting expectations and enticing readers to invest in your characters and their journey.

The introduction of your lead characters should be done in a way that highlights their complexity and the stakes involved in their story. *In "Eleanor Oliphant Is Completely Fine"* by Gail Honeyman, Eleanor's quirky and structured life is established early on, giving readers a clear sense of her character before the plot deepens. Similarly, your billionaire protagonist and their love interest should be introduced in scenarios that showcase their personalities, desires, and the initial obstacles they face. Whether it's a glimpse into the billionaire's high-powered world or a moment that reveals the love interest's aspirations or challenges, these early scenes are pivotal for building empathy and interest.

As you move into the heart of your story, focus on developing the relationship between your billionaire and their love interest through escalating conflicts and deepening emotional connections. *"Outlander"* by Diana Gabaldon masterfully balances romantic development with tension as Claire and Jamie navigate time travel and war. Each challenge they face not only tests their love but also reveals new layers of their characters. Apply this principle by crafting obstacles directly tied to your protagonists' fears or flaws, ensuring their journey toward love is neither smooth nor predictable but always compelling.

The midpoint of your story should act as a turning point, dramatically altering the relationship dynamics or the characters' goals. In *"Gone Girl"* by Gillian Flynn, the midpoint reveals a major plot twist that changes everything the reader thought they knew about the characters and their motivations. For your billionaire romance, this could be a revelation about the protagonist's past, a significant setback in their relationship, or a decision that jeopardizes their future. This moment should challenge the characters and the reader, setting the stage for the developments that follow.

Building towards the climax, your narrative should weave together the various plot threads and character arcs, increasing tension and anticipation. "*The Seven Husbands of Evelyn Hugo*" by Taylor Jenkins Reid does this by deepening mysteries and relationships, leading to a powerful revelation. Similarly, your story should escalate the stakes through personal dilemmas, external threats, or a combination of both, pushing your characters to their limits and forcing them to confront their deepest fears and desires.

The climax itself is the moment of the highest emotional intensity and should satisfyingly resolve the central conflict. *"Big Little Lies"* by Liane Moriarty culminates in a dramatic confrontation that brings all the story's tensions to a head, offering resolution and understanding. In your billionaire romance, this might mean a grand gesture of love that overcomes the final obstacle or a confrontation that clears up misunderstandings, solidifying the bond between your protagonists in a way that feels earned and true to their characters.

Following the climax, your story should move into an outcome where the aftermath of the climax is explored, and the characters' lives start to stabilize. *"Normal People"* by

Sally Rooney provides a closer look at how its protagonists come to terms with their relationship and individual growth after the story's emotional peak. This section is your opportunity to show the growth of your billionaire and their love interest, highlighting how they've changed and what they've learned. It's also a chance to tie up loose ends, ensuring that secondary plotlines and characters are given proper closure.

The conclusion of your billionaire romance should leave readers with a sense of satisfaction and reflection. It's not just about providing a happy ending but about reinforcing your story's themes and emotional journey. *"The Rosie Project"* by Graeme Simsion ends on a hopeful note that reflects the growth of its characters and the power of love to overcome obstacles. Your story's ending should similarly resonate, leaving readers with lasting impressions of your characters' journey and the world you've built. Whether through a poignant final scene or a look into the future, ensure your conclusion offers closure and a rewarding payoff for your readers' investment in the story.

Chapter 14

Balancing Subplots

In crafting a billionaire romance, your primary storyline captures the heart of your readers, but it's the subplots that add the necessary layers to make your narrative truly stand out. Think of your novel like a garden. Your romance is the central, most spectacular flower, but the surrounding plants —the subplots—create a setting that allows your main story to shine even brighter. These additional narratives should complement, not compete with, the romance. For instance, in *"The Proposal"* by Jasmine Guillory, the subplot of the protagonist's career struggles provides depth to her character. It adds stakes to the romantic storyline, enriching the narrative without overshadowing the central romance.

Subplots offer a chance to explore themes that might not fit into the leading storyline but are still relevant to your characters' world. They can act as a mirror or contrast to the primary romance, shedding light on different aspects of love or challenging the protagonists' beliefs and growth. For example, a subplot involving the best friend's romantic journey can highlight what the leading characters fear or desire in their relationship. This technique, used effectively in *"Beach Read"* by Emily Henry, deepens the reader's understanding of the leading characters and keeps the narrative engaging across multiple fronts.

Character development is another area where subplots can shine. They allow secondary characters to have their moments, making the world of your novel feel populated with real, complex individuals. These characters' journeys can parallel or intersect with the primary romance in meaningful ways, providing lessons or support to the protagonists. A subplot focusing on a family member overcoming a personal challenge, as seen in *"Crazy Rich Asians"* by Kevin Kwan, can offer moments of growth and reflection for the leading characters, enhancing the emotional richness of the story.

Your subplots should also serve to increase tension and stakes within the narrative. They can introduce external conflicts or obstacles that the leading characters must navigate, indirectly testing their relationship. For instance, a business rivalry subplot adds excitement and intrigue and challenges the billionaire protagonist's priorities and values, pushing them towards personal growth that affects their romantic relationship. This dynamic is skillfully handled in

"The Hating Game" by Sally Thorne, where professional competition adds a delicious layer of tension to the romance.

Pacing is crucial when balancing subplots with the leading romance. Introduce and resolve these additional narratives at a pace that keeps readers engaged without overwhelming them. The key is to weave these stories in and out of the leading romance at moments that enhance the primary narrative rather than detract from it. A subplot about a secret from the past that is gradually revealed can add suspense and depth, driving readers to keep turning the pages in anticipation of both the romantic and subplot resolutions.

Subplots offer an opportunity to expand the world of your novel. You can explore the setting, social backdrop, or cultural context that influences your characters' lives and decisions through them. This broader view can make your billionaire romance feel more grounded and relatable, providing a backdrop against which the romance shines even brighter. In *"Red, White & Royal Blue"* by Casey McQuiston, the political subplot adds depth to the characters' world. It raises the stakes of their romance, making their relationship all the more compelling.

Balance in tone between your leading romance and subplots is also essential. If your central story is intense and dramatic, a lighter, humorous subplot can give readers relief and variety. This contrast can enhance the emotional impact of both the romance and the subplot, as seen in *"Attach-ments"* by Rainbow Rowell, where the humorous tone of the email exchanges contrasts with and highlights the deeper emotional journey of the protagonists.

Subplots can also be used to build suspense and foreshadow events in the leading romance. Clues or challenges presented in a subplot might later play a crucial role in developing or resolving the central love story. This technique can keep readers guessing and engaged, eagerly piecing together how each narrative thread will tie back to the primary romance.

The resolution of your subplots should feel satisfying and contribute to the overall conclusion of your novel. Each should come to a close before or as part of the climax of the primary romance, ensuring that the final chapters focus on resolving the central love story. This approach, ensuring that no narrative thread is left dangling, provides a sense of closure and completeness to your story, as demonstrated in *"One Day in December"* by Josie Silver, where subplots wrap up in a way that enriches the ending of the primary romance.

Consider how your subplots intertwine with the primary romance when revising your manuscript. Ask yourself whether they add value through character development, tension, or world-building. If a subplot doesn't serve the story, consider cutting or revising it. This editing process is crucial for maintaining a focused and engaging narrative.

Remember, the best subplots are those that, while they could stand on their own, are better for being part of your novel. They should feel integral to the story, enriching the tapestry of your narrative without overwhelming the main thread of romance. A well-crafted subplot, like those in *"Evvie Drake Starts Over"* by Linda Holmes, feels essential to the story, contributing to the novel's themes and emotional journey.

Finally, don't forget to use feedback from beta readers and writing groups to gauge the effectiveness of your subplots. Sometimes, what makes perfect sense in your head might not translate as clearly on the page. Fresh eyes can help you see where a subplot might overshadow the romance or where additional development could enhance the story. This feedback is invaluable for achieving the delicate balance required to make your billionaire romance novel a satisfying and compelling read.

Chapter 15

Crafting Steamy Scenes

Crafting steamy scenes in a billionaire romance requires a delicate touch, ensuring they enhance the narrative without overwhelming it. Begin by focusing on the emotional connection between your characters. This depth elevates a scene from merely physical to genuinely passionate and memorable. The anticipation and tension leading up to these moments are crucial; they should simmer throughout your narrative, making the culmination of this tension all the more satisfying. The emotional buildup, the shared looks, and the unspoken words lay the groundwork for a scene that resonates with readers on a deeper level.

When writing these scenes, descriptive language is your ally. Opt for imagery and metaphors that evoke a sense of place, emotion, and sensation, painting a picture that engages the reader's senses. The aim is to create an immersive experience that captures the intensity of the moment while leaving enough to the imagination. This approach allows readers to become co-creators in the experience, filling in the details with their own imagination, which can make the scene more impactful and personal to them.

Dialogue within steamy scenes can significantly amplify their intensity. The characters' exchange can be a powerful tool to convey desire, deepen their connection, and reveal vulnerabilities. Whether it's playful teasing or deep confessions, what the characters say—or don't say—can add layers to the scene, making it about more than just physical attraction. This dialogue can transform a simple encounter into a pivotal moment in their relationship, showcasing their compatibility and mutual desire.

Finding the right level of heat involves understanding your audience and the tone of your novel. The steaminess of a scene should align with the expectations set by the narrative and the characters' development. A sudden explicit scene in a narrative that has been more subdued or romantic can jar the reader, breaking the story's spell. Matching these scenes' intensity to the romance's overall arc ensures they enhance rather than detract from the story.

Pacing is vital in balancing the steamy scenes with the broader narrative. These moments should feel like a natural progression of the characters' relationship, adding to their emotional journey rather than pausing it. Introduce steamy scenes at moments that escalate the relationship in a meaningful way, using them as milestones that mark a deepening of the characters' connection and understanding of each other.

The language you choose plays a significant role in setting the heat level. Opt for words and descriptions that evoke the sensuality and emotion of the moment without crossing into territory that might make your readers uncomfortable. Striking the right balance often involves focusing on the characters' sensations and emotional responses rather than providing a mechanical account of their actions. Eloquent and evocative language can create steamy, sophisticated, and hot scenes.

Consider the unique settings your billionaire romance offers for these scenes. The world of affluence opens up possibilities for encounters in exotic locales or high-end environments that can add an element of fantasy and escape. However, ensure these settings also reflect the characters' personalities and the story's mood, making the scenes feel grounded in the narrative and not just added for spectacle.

Steamy scenes should also contribute to the story's emotional arc and character development. Beyond the physical connection, these moments can reveal insights into the characters' fears, hopes, and desires. They can act as turning points where characters confront their feelings or make significant decisions, seamlessly integrating the scenes into the narrative's fabric.

Varying the intensity and style of steamy scenes throughout your novel can keep readers engaged and the narrative dynamic. Not every intimate moment needs to be described in detail; sometimes, the suggestion or aftermath of a scene can be just as powerful. This variation keeps the narrative fresh and allows for a range of emotional experiences between the characters.

The aftermath of these scenes is crucial for character development and the progression of the romance. How characters reflect on these moments can provide insight into their emotional state and the dynamics of their relationship. It's an opportunity to explore the impact of their intimacy on their personal growth and the story at large, reinforcing the significance of these encounters beyond the physical.

Writing steamy scenes requires balancing being true to your characters and pushing them beyond their comfort zones. Their interactions should feel authentic to who they are and where they are in their relationship. If a scene feels forced or out of character, it risks pulling readers out of the story. Trusting your understanding of the characters will guide you in creating genuine and exhilarating scenes.

Feedback from beta readers or critique partners can be invaluable in gauging the effectiveness of your steamy scenes. They can provide insights into whether these moments enhance the narrative and resonate emotionally or if they feel gratuitous. Use this feedback to refine your scenes, ensuring they contribute to the romance and the story's overall impact.

Revisiting and revising steamy scenes is as important as any other part of your writing process. With each draft, assess whether these moments advance the romance, deepen character development, and fit within the narrative's pacing. Editing with a critical eye ensures that each scene serves the story, maintaining the delicate balance between passion and plot and ultimately delivering a romance that captivates and satisfies your readers.

By adhering to these guidelines, you can craft steamy scenes that not only sizzle but also deepen the emotional connection between your characters, enriching your billionaire romance with tasteful and intensely passionate moments.

Chapter 16

The Role of Secondary Characters

In crafting a billionaire romance, secondary characters play pivotal roles that extend far beyond mere background presence. They serve as catalysts for plot development, offering the main characters challenges and opportunities for growth. For instance, in *"Bared to You"* by Sylvia Day, the protagonist's best friend, Cary Taylor, provides comic relief and emotional support, highlighting the protagonist's vulnerabilities and strengths. Secondary characters like Cary can mirror the internal conflicts of the main characters, providing a sounding board for their fears and desires. Their interactions enrich the narrative, adding complexity and realism to the story.

Secondary characters often drive the main characters closer together or pull them apart, creating tension and conflict within the romance. In *"The Bridgerton Series"* by Julia

Quinn, siblings and friends play significant roles in match-making, misunderstandings, and reconciliations, directly influencing the romantic outcomes. These characters can act as obstacles or allies, pushing the main characters to confront their feelings and make difficult decisions. Their actions and decisions can significantly impact the trajectory of the romance, making them indispensable to the narrative.

The family members of your billionaire protagonist can offer a unique window into their background and values. For example, in *"Crazy Rich Asians"* by Kevin Kwan, Nick Young's family, with their expectations and traditions, provides a rich backdrop against which his relationship with Rachel Chu unfolds. Family dynamics can reveal why the billionaire behaves in specific ways in romantic contexts, offering readers a deeper understanding of their motivations and fears. These relationships can also introduce conflicts that challenge the billionaire's priorities and decisions in love.

Work colleagues and rivals introduce another dimension to the billionaire romance narrative. They can embody the professional challenges and ambitions of the protagonist, as seen in *"The Hating Game"* by Sally Thorne. Colleagues like Joshua Templeman provide a competitive dynamic and serve as a measure of personal growth for Lucy Hutton. Work-related subplots involving these characters can parallel the lead romance, highlighting themes of rivalry, ambition, and partnership.

Friends of the love interest are crucial in grounding the story in reality. They offer perspectives outside the whirl-wind billionaire lifestyle, reminding the love interest (and the reader) of the world beyond the romance. In *"Me Before You"* by Jojo Moyes, Louisa's family and friend Treena contrast Will's world, emphasizing Louisa's sacrifices and changes. These characters underscore the transformative power of love, supporting the love interest's journey and highlighting the stakes involved.

Mentors and father figures can provide wisdom and guidance to the main characters, steering them through personal and professional dilemmas. In *"The Seven Husbands of Evelyn Hugo"* by Taylor Jenkins Reid, Harry Cameron acts as a moral compass and confidant to Evelyn, influencing her decisions in life and love. Such characters can impart lessons from their own experiences, offering the protagonists valuable insights that aid their emotional growth.

Antagonists and villains in the narrative serve to test the strength and resilience of the main characters' relationship. Through their schemes and obstacles, they create situations that force the protagonists to fight for their love. For example, in *"It Ends with Us"* by Colleen Hoover, Ryle Kincaid presents a complex challenge to Lily Bloom, pushing her to confront brutal truths and make heart-wrenching decisions. These characters highlight the protagonists' courage and determination, making their journey towards happiness all the more rewarding.

Whether related to the main characters or part of the broader narrative, children bring out the protagonists' softer, more nurturing sides. Their innocence and straightforwardness can cut through the complexities of adult relationships, offering moments of clarity and truth. In *"Sustained"* by Emma Chase, Jake Becker's nieces and nephews become central to his relationship with Chelsea McQuaid, revealing his capacity for love and commitment.

Ex-partners and old flames reintroduce past conflicts and unresolved feelings, complicating the current romance. Their presence can reignite jealousy, insecurity, or reflection, as seen in *"Second Chance Summer"* by Jill Shalvis. These characters force the main characters to confront their history, offering them a chance to grow and choose a different path.

In some narratives, secondary characters who start as minor figures can grow in importance, reflecting the dynamic nature of relationships. As the story progresses, their interactions with the main characters can reveal new facets of the protagonists' personalities or introduce subplots that enrich the narrative. This evolution mirrors real life, where people who once seemed peripheral can become central to our lives.

The setting of the billionaire romance itself can be personified through its inhabitants, who collectively contribute to the atmosphere and social norms that influence the protagonists. In *"Pride and Prejudice"* by Jane Austen, the residents of Meryton and their gossip play a significant role in shaping the social pressures and opportunities for Elizabeth Bennet and Mr. Darcy. These characters add depth to the setting, making it a living, breathing aspect of the story.

The portrayal of secondary characters should be multidimensional, avoiding stereotypes to ensure they contribute meaningfully to the story. They should have their own goals, flaws, and growth arcs that, while not as prominent as the lead characters', still resonate with the reader. This approach ensures that the world of your billionaire romance feels populated with characters who are compelling in their own right.

Secondary characters can also serve as foils to the main characters, highlighting certain traits or choices by contrast. In *"The Great Gatsby"* by F. Scott Fitzgerald, the guests at Gatsby's parties contrast with Gatsby's isolation and unfulfilled desires, emphasizing the themes of longing and the facade of the American Dream. Through these contrasts, secondary characters can sharpen the focus on the main characters' journeys.

Humorous sidekicks or quirky friends can provide comic relief, balancing the tension and drama of the romance. Their lighthearted moments and witty commentary can offer readers a reprieve from the emotional intensity of the main storyline. In *"To All the Boys I've Loved Before"* by Jenny

Han, Lara Jean's friend Chris offers a humorous counter-point to Lara Jean's romantic dilemmas, adding fun and charm to the story.

Secondary characters offer opportunities for spin-offs or sequels, allowing the world you've created to expand beyond the original narrative. Readers often become attached to these characters, and their stories can provide fresh perspectives on your crafted world. This approach enriches the universe of your billionaire romance and keeps your readers engaged and eager for more.

By carefully considering the role of secondary characters in your billionaire romance, you ensure that your narrative is rich, layered, and engaging. These characters add complexity to the story, providing challenges, support, and depth that make your primary romance all the more compelling.

Chapter 17

Avoid Common Mistakes

Avoiding common mistakes is crucial for creating a story that captivates and resonates with readers. One of the first pitfalls to avoid is creating a billionaire character who is nothing more than their wealth. Depth, vulnerabilities, and complexities make characters relatable and intriguing. Your billionaire should have passions, flaws, and a backstory that shapes their actions and decisions, making them more than just a wallet with legs. This approach ensures your character is multidimensional and engages readers more deeply.

Another mistake is overlooking the importance of research. Whether it's understanding the finer details of high mainte-nance, the lifestyle of the rich and famous, or the intricacies of the businesses they run, accurate depiction is critical. Misrepresentations can break the spell of believability you're weaving for your audience. For example, inaccurately portraying the inner workings of a tech billionaire's empire can alienate readers familiar with the sector. Diligent research underpins a believable and immersive world for your characters to inhabit.

Falling into the trap of instant love without developing the relationship can also diminish the impact of your story. Building a believable romance requires time, with characters learning about each other and facing challenges together. This development is what makes the eventual union satisfying. Instant attraction is a staple of romance, but the deepening of this initial spark into love should be shown through shared experiences, conflicts, and resolutions that test and strengthen their bond.

Neglecting the love interest's development is another common oversight. Just as the billionaire protagonist requires depth, so too does their partner. The love interest should have its own goals, challenges, and growth throughout the story, not existing solely in response to the billionaire. A well-rounded love interest with aspirations and complexities contributes to a balanced and compelling narrative, making the romance more believable and engaging.

Overusing clichés and tropes without a fresh twist can make your story stale and predictable. While tropes are a foundational element of romance writing, adding unique elements or subverting expectations can breathe new life into familiar scenarios. For example, instead of the typical rescue scenario, perhaps the billionaire needs saving, either literally or metaphorically, by the love interest. This inversion can offer new dynamics and keep readers intrigued.

Ignoring the potential for conflict within the billionaire's world is a missed opportunity to add depth to your story. The lifestyle of the wealthy can bring its own set of challenges and pressures, from public scrutiny to the isolation that can accompany extreme wealth. Integrating these elements as obstacles in your romance can provide realism and complexity, enriching the narrative and offering more avenues for character growth.

Another common mistake is failing to create a believable world for your characters. The settings, from luxurious estates to exclusive events, should be vividly described and consistent with the characters' lifestyles. However, balancing this with moments of normalcy and relatability is crucial, ensuring that the world feels grounded and natural, not just a fantasy playground.

Allowing the wealth aspect to solve all problems in the narrative can undermine the story's tension and the characters' growth. Challenges faced by the characters should require more than just a financial fix, emphasizing personal development, emotional intelligence, and the power of human connection as solutions. This approach ensures the story has meaningful stakes and keeps readers invested in the characters' journey.

Overlooking the need for the billionaire to evolve as a character can result in a stagnant narrative. The billionaire's wealth shouldn't shield them from personal growth; their experiences and relationship with the love interest should prompt introspection and change. This evolution transforms the romance from a simple love story into a tale of transformative connection.

Relying too heavily on external conflicts without developing internal ones can lead to a lack of emotional depth. While external challenges drive the plot, the characters' internal struggles, such as fears, insecurities, and ambitions, resonate with readers. Balancing internal and external conflicts enriches the narrative, making the characters' victories more satisfying.

Forgetting to give secondary characters their arcs and purposes can make the world around the main characters feel flat. These characters should add to the story's richness, offering support, conflict, or comic relief. They can also reflect or contrast the lead romance, providing depth and complexity to the narrative landscape.

Assuming that all readers are looking for the same level of steaminess in their romance can alienate parts of your audience. It's essential to consider the tone and audience of your novel when writing intimate scenes. Balancing sensuality with emotion ensures that these moments contribute to the characters' relationship development rather than serving as gratuitous content.

Not providing a satisfying resolution for both the primary romance and the subplots can leave readers feeling unresolved. Each narrative thread introduced, no matter how minor, should be tied up by the story's end, offering closure and a sense of completeness. This attention to detail shows respect for your readers and enhances their enjoyment of the story.

Underestimating the importance of a well-crafted ending is a significant misstep. The conclusion of your billionaire romance should resolve the central conflict and leave readers with a lasting impression of the characters' journey. A memorable ending can transform a good story into one readers recommend enthusiastically, ensuring your novel's place in their hearts.

By avoiding these common pitfalls, you can craft a billionaire romance that stands out for its depth, realism, and emotional resonance. Each element of your story, from character development to world-building, contributes to creating a narrative that captivates and satisfies your readers, marking your work as not just another romance but a memorable exploration of love and transformation.

Chapter 18

Editing

Editing and polishing your manuscript are crucial steps in bringing your billionaire romance novel from a rough draft to a polished, ready-to-publish work. This stage is where you refine your story, fix any inconsistencies, and enhance your narrative's flow. It's not just about correcting grammar and spelling errors; it's an opportunity to deepen character development, tighten pacing, and ensure your plot points are compelling and logical. Think of this phase as the final dress rehearsal before your book's debut, where every element of your story must be scrutinized and perfected. This meticulous attention to detail will significantly impact your manuscript's quality, making it more engaging and enjoyable for your readers.

Self-editing techniques can significantly improve the quality of your manuscript before it ever reaches a beta reader or professional editor. One effective method is to put your manuscript aside for a few weeks after you've finished writing. This short break allows you to return to your work with fresh eyes and a new perspective, making it easier to spot issues you might have overlooked. Reading your manuscript aloud is another powerful technique, as it can help you catch awkward phrasing, repetitive language, and dialogue that doesn't sound natural. Additionally, using software tools designed to catch grammatical errors and suggest improvements can be helpful, but remember, these tools are not infallible and should not replace careful, personal review.

The importance of beta readers cannot be overstated. These early readers provide valuable feedback from the perspective of your target audience. They can point out confusing parts of your story, highlight characters that aren't resonating, and suggest areas where the pacing might lag. Choose beta readers familiar with your genre and represent your ideal reader demographic. Their insights will be crucial in identifying the strengths and weaknesses of your manuscript, allowing you to make necessary adjustments before proceeding to professional editing.

Professional editors play a pivotal role in the journey of your manuscript from draft to publication. Unlike beta readers, professional editors bring technical expertise in grammar, syntax, and narrative structure to the table. They can help you elevate your writing, ensuring that your manuscript is error-free and polished to a high shine. There are different types of editing to consider, including developmental editing for big-picture issues, copy editing for line-by-line corrections, and proofreading for a final check. Investing in a professional editor is an investment in the quality of your book, significantly enhancing its readability and appeal.

Preparing your manuscript for submission to agents or publishers requires careful attention to submission guidelines. Each agent or publisher may have specific requirements regarding formatting, document type, and the information to be included in your submission package. This often consists of a query letter, a synopsis, and a defined portion of your manuscript. Tailoring each submission to meet these guidelines is crucial; failure to do so can result in your manuscript being dismissed without consideration. This preparation phase is also an excellent time to refine your query letter and synopsis, ensuring they are as compelling as your manuscript.

If you're leaning towards self-publishing, preparing your manuscript involves a different set of considerations. Ensuring your manuscript is professionally edited is just as crucial in this route as self-published works directly compete with traditionally published books. Formatting your manuscript for various self-publishing platforms can be complex, as each platform may have its own set of requirements. Additionally, you'll need to think about cover design, ISBN acquisition, and setting up your book on the chosen publishing platforms. Self-publishing gives you complete control over the process, but it also means taking on all the responsibilities typically handled by traditional publishers.

Regardless of your chosen publishing path, the importance of editing and polishing your manuscript cannot be understated. A well-edited book reflects your dedication to your craft and respect for your readers. It's the final, critical step in ensuring the story you've poured your heart into is presented in the best possible light. Whether through self-editing, feedback from beta readers, the expertise of professional editors, or the careful preparation for submission or self-publishing, each step in this process is a building block toward creating a memorable and successful billionaire romance novel. Remember, the effort you put into editing and polishing your manuscript is a direct investment in your book's potential to captivate and enchant your readers.

Chapter 19

Marketing Your Book

Marketing your billionaire romance is a task that begins long before the book hits the shelves or online platforms. It's a strategic process that involves understanding who your readers are, what they desire, and how best to reach them. A successful marketing campaign will make your book stand out in a crowded genre, enticing readers with the promise of luxury, intrigue, and heart-fluttering romance. This process includes creating a captivating cover, crafting a compelling blurb, ensuring the first chapter grabs attention, and implementing effective promotional strategies. Each step is designed to draw readers into the world you've created, making them eager to dive into the story of your billionaire protagonist and their journey toward love.

Understanding your market and audience is crucial in the competitive landscape of billionaire romance novels.

Readers of this genre often look for escapism, thrilling plots, and characters they can root for or fall in love with. They might be drawn to the fantasy of luxury and power but stay for the emotional depth and the transformative journey of love. To connect with this audience, you must dive deep into what makes billionaire romances appealing—be it the Cinderella-esque stories, the tension-filled love affairs, or the fairy-tale endings. Engaging with your audience through social media, reading reviews, and participating in romance fiction forums can provide invaluable insights into their preferences and expectations.

Your cover is often the first point of contact between your book and potential readers. It needs to strike the perfect balance between genre expectations and unique appeal. A well-designed cover communicates the essence of your story at a glance, promising readers the kind of experience they seek in a billionaire romance. Luxurious imagery, coupled with fonts that evoke elegance and intrigue, can make your book stand out. Investing in professional cover design is crucial because, in the world of book sales, appearances are not just superficial—they're everything.

Your blurb acts as a bridge between the curiosity sparked by your cover and the decision to purchase or read more. It should be enticing, teasing the drama, romance, and stakes without giving away too much. A good blurb introduces your billionaire protagonist and their love interest, sets up the conflict, and hints at the transformational journey ahead.

This brief ad copy needs to capture the essence of your story and the emotional rollercoaster that awaits, encouraging readers to take the plunge into your narrative world.

The importance of your strong first chapter cannot be overstated. This is your opportunity to hook the reader with your writing style, the allure of your characters, and the promise of an engaging story. Your opening should set the tone for the rest of the book, introduce key characters engagingly, and start weaving the tantalizing web of your plot. The first chapter is where you make your first impression, and in the world of billionaire romance, it's essential to captivate your readers from the very beginning.

Strategies for launching and promoting your book should be multifaceted and begin well before the actual release date. Creating anticipation is key. This can be achieved through cover reveals, teaser excerpts, and pre-order options. Establishing a launch team of dedicated beta readers who can help spread the word about your book and give you feedback before your launch is also invaluable. These early promotional efforts can build momentum leading up to your launch, ensuring your book debuts to an audience ready and eager to dive in.

Social media is a powerful tool for connecting with readers and promoting your book. Platforms like Instagram, TikTok, and Facebook allow you to share visually appealing content, updates about your writing process, and special promotions.

Engaging with your followers by responding to comments and participating in genre-specific hashtags or groups can help you build a community of fans who are invested in your work.

Email marketing remains one of the most effective ways to reach your audience directly. A well-targeted newsletter informs your readers about upcoming releases, exclusive content, and behind-the-scenes glimpses into your writing life. Offering something of value, such as a free short story or a sneak peek at an upcoming chapter, can encourage sign-ups and keep subscribers engaged.

Reaching out to book bloggers, influencers, and book reviewers specializing in your genre can significantly boost your novel's visibility. Positive reviews from trusted sources can lend credibility to your book and introduce it to wider audiences. Personalized pitches, offering review copies known as ARCs, and being open to podcast interviews can foster relationships with influencers who can champion your book.

Whether virtual or in-person, book signings and author events offer a personal touch to your promotional efforts. These events allow you to connect with readers, share your inspiration for the book, and generate excitement. Even on TikTok, the personal connection forged through these events can turn casual readers into loyal fans.

Participating in book fairs and literary festivals can also widen your reach. These events attract book lovers and allow you to showcase your work, network with other authors, and engage with potential readers face-to-face. Being present in these literary communities can elevate your profile and introduce your billionaire romance to new audiences.

Running promotions and giveaways effectively garner attention and entice readers to give your book a chance. Limited-time free and 99-cent promotions, ARC giveaways on TikTok, or reviews on platforms like BookFunnel, Book-Sirens, and Booksprouts can create buzz around your book. These strategies help increase visibility and encourage word-of-mouth recommendations, further amplifying your book's reach.

Paid advertising, through platforms like Amazon Ads, BookBub, or Facebook, can target potential readers based on specific interests, browsing habits, or previous purchases. A well-crafted ad campaign can drive traffic to your book's online listings, increasing sales and visibility. However, it's important to monitor the performance of your ads and adjust your strategy as needed to ensure a good return on investment.

Building partnerships with other authors in the billionaire romance genre can open up cross-promotion opportunities. Collaborating on box sets, participating in group giveaways, or co-hosting virtual events can introduce your book to the established audiences of your fellow authors. These partnerships can be mutually beneficial, expanding your reach and bringing new readers to your work.

Engaging with your readers and seeking feedback can help your future marketing strategies. Understanding what resonated with your audience—or what didn't—can help you refine your approach for your next release. Maintaining an open dialogue with your readers keeps them invested in your work and can turn casual readers into lifelong fans.

By employing these strategies thoughtfully and consistently, you can effectively market your billionaire romance novel, ensuring it captures the hearts of readers eager for stories of love, luxury, and emotional depth. Marketing is an ongoing process that requires patience, persistence, and a deep understanding of your target audience. With the right approach, you can build a strong foundation for your book's success and establish yourself as a beloved author in the billionaire romance genre.

Chapter 20

Afterword

As you stand on the brink of completing your billionaire romance novel, remember that the journey you've undertaken is a testament to your courage, creativity, and dedication to storytelling. Crafting a narrative that captures the complexities of love, power, and redemption is no small feat. It requires not just talent but a steadfast commitment to exploring the depths of human emotion and desire. Let the challenges you've faced along the way not be seen as obstacles but as stepping stones that have shaped you into a more skilled and empathetic storyteller. Each word you've written, each character you've brought to life, has contributed to the rich tapestry of your narrative, making it uniquely yours.

In this final stretch, it's crucial to nurture the belief in your voice and the stories you wish to tell. The world of billionaire romance is vast and varied, enriched by each new perspective that dares to reimagine its boundaries. Trust in the power of your narrative, in the characters that have whispered their secrets to you in the quiet moments of creation. Your story is a beacon of possibility, a reminder that in the realm of fiction, there are infinite ways to explore the themes of love and aspiration.

Remember, the act of writing is, in itself, an act of courage. You've poured your heart into the pages, baring your soul in the hopes of touching the hearts of others. As you prepare to share your work with the world, do so with the confidence that comes from knowing you've given your all to this endeavor. Whether traditional or self-published, the path to publication is fraught with its own challenges, but you are equipped to face them. Each rejection, each critique, is but a signpost guiding you toward becoming a more adept and resilient author.

Embrace the community of writers and readers that surrounds you. A writer's journey is often solitary, but the connections we forge through our stories sustain us. Seek out fellow authors, engage with your readers, and immerse yourself in the conversations that animate the world of romance writing. These relationships will be your anchor and inspiration, reminding you of the impact your words can have on the lives of others.

Never lose sight of the joy that writing brings. There will be days of doubt and frustration when the words seem just out of reach. In these times, remember why you embarked on this journey: the thrill of creation, the love of storytelling, and the desire to share a piece of your soul with the world. Your passion is the most powerful tool in your arsenal—guard it, nurture it, and let it guide you as you continue to write, explore, and dream. The world awaits your stories, and only you can tell them.

9 781925 988857